| OC 4'93 | DATE DUE | | JY 30'08 |
|---|---|---|---|
| OC 23 '93 | JAN 30 '96 | OC 04 '99 | |
| JUN 24 '94 | JUN 12 '96 | JY 24 '00 | JY 07 '14 |
| JUL 28 '99 | JUL 08 '96 | AG 03 '00 | |
| NOV 25 '94 | JUL 12 '96 | SE 14 '00 | JY 08 '15 |
| MAR 08 '95 | MAR 67 '97 | OC 11 '01 | |
| MAR 22 '95 | JUL 03 '97 | JY 02 '02 | |
| JUN 13 '95 | AUG 28 '97 | JY 15 '04 | |
| AUG 14 '95 | JUN 25 '98 | JY 29 '04 | |
| Aug 95 | JUL 15 '98 | NO 14 '05 | |
| OCT 09 '95 | AUG 05 '98 | JY 12 '06 | |
| OCT 26 '95 | SEP 23 '98 | AG 21 '07 | |

E
Mar        Martin, Rodney
           There's a dinosaur in
           the park!

# THERE'S A

# DINOSAUR

## IN THE PARK!

A Quality Time™ Book

**Library of Congress Cataloging-in-Publication Data**

Martin,Rodney.
  There's a dinosaur in the park!

  (A Quality time book)
  Summary: A young boy's imagination brings to life a
dinosaur playmate in the park.
  [1. Dinosaurs—Fiction.    2. Imagination—Fiction.
3. Play—Fiction]   1. Siow, John, ill.   II. Title.
PZ7.M364184Th   1987    [E]     86-42811
ISBN 1-55532-176-3
ISBN 1-55532-151-8 (lib. bdg.)

North American edition first published in 1987 by

Gareth Stevens, Inc.
7221 West Green Tree Road
Milwaukee, WI 53223, USA

Text copyright © 1980 by Rodney Martin
Illustrations copyright © 1980 by John Siow

First published in Australia by Era Publications.

Typeset by A-Line Typographers, Milwaukee.
Cover design: Laurie Shock.

1  2  3  4  5  6  7  8  9  92  91  90  89  88  87

# THERE'S A DINOSAUR IN THE PARK!

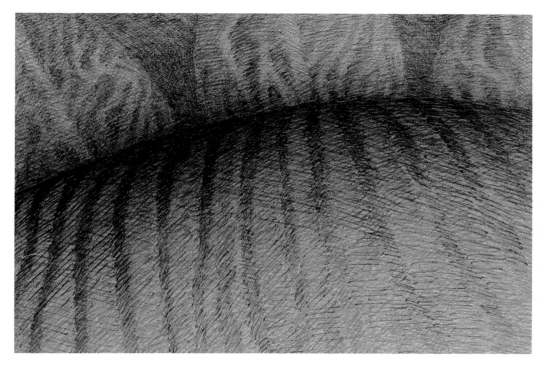

Story by Rodney Martin
Pictures by John Siow

Gareth Stevens Publishing
Milwaukee

Hey! There's a dinosaur in the park!

I've seen him.
He lives in the bushes,
where it's dark.

He's got fierce eyes.
And he's got dagger claws.
And he's got spikes sticking out
all up and down his back.
He's SCARY.

9

He's got a DANGEROUS dinosaur tail
and a giant jaw
full of crunching teeth.

He looked hungry,
so I threw an old soda can
right into his mouth.

13

He ate it!
So I gave him some paper
and some more cans
and some boxes and things.
And he ate them, too.
He eats ANYTHING.

I touched his spikes.
Did he mind?

He didn't bite me.
So I climbed onto his tail
and up on his back,
and I sat on him.
He let me!
Then he stamped his sharp dagger claws.
And he showed his crunching teeth
and went "RRR-R-A-A-AAH!"
He was FEROCIOUS.

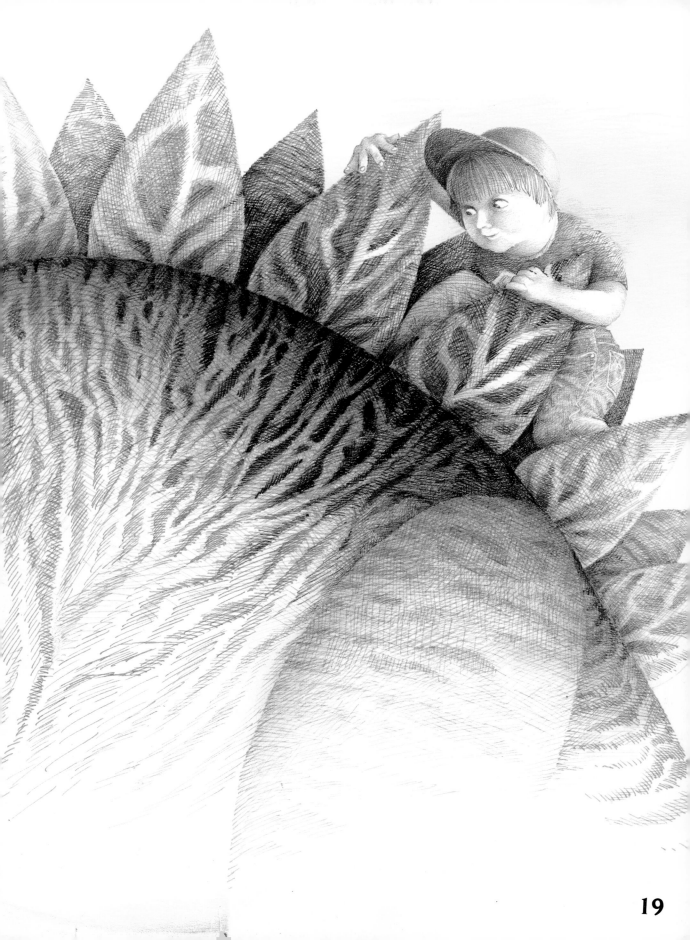

19

Watch out!

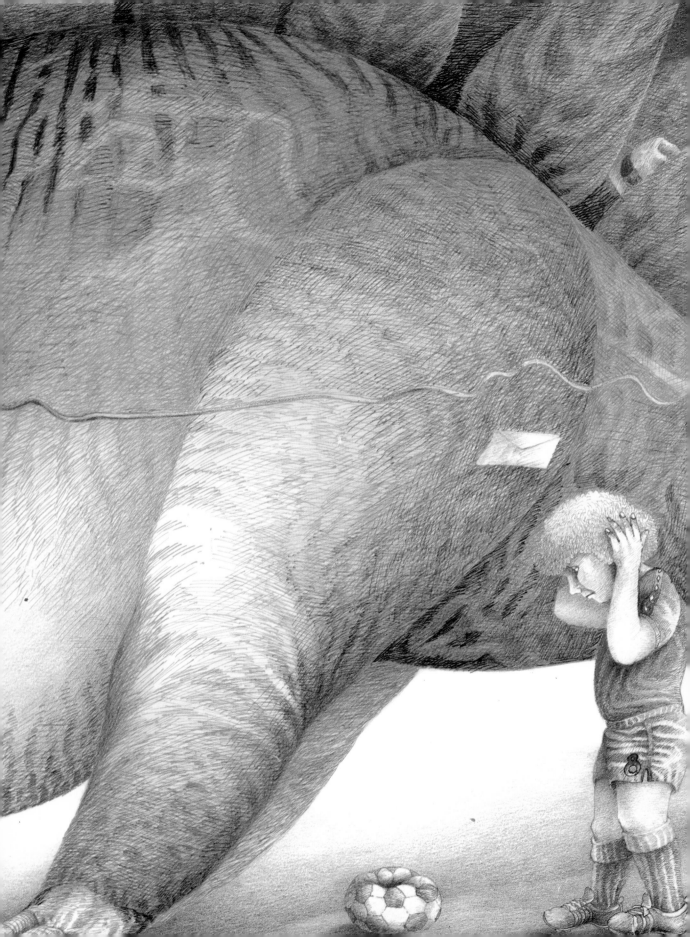

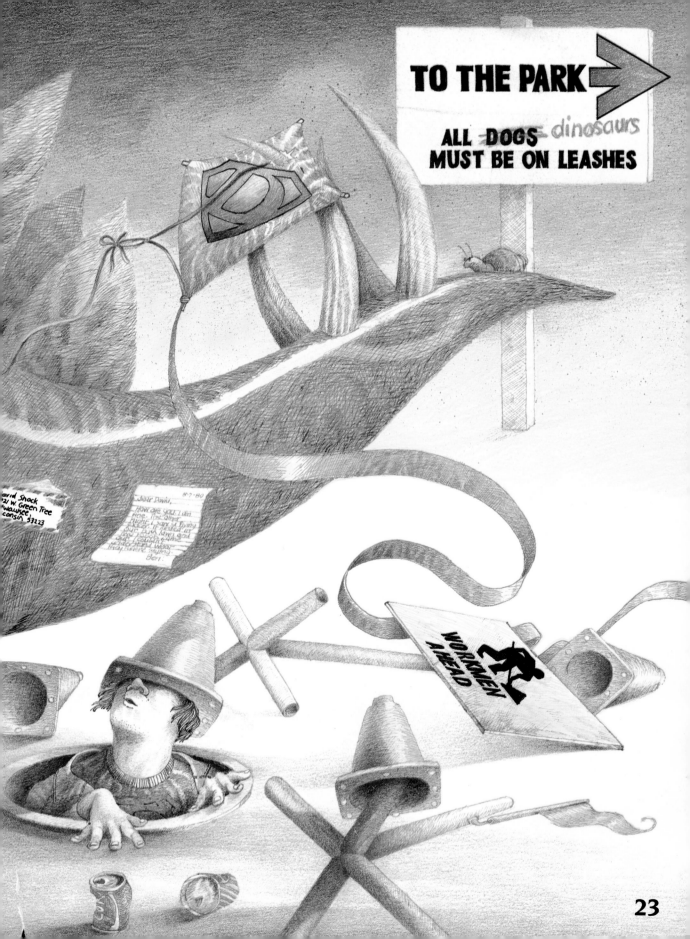

But I'm not scared of him.
No I'm not.

I even went
"RRR-R-A-A-AAH!" at him.

But he didn't chase ME.
He just stayed in the park.

I just MIGHT see that dinosaur again —
tomorrow.